PAIR-IT BOOKS

The Princess and the Castle

Written by Alice Leonhardt
Illustrated by John Courtney

STECK-VAUGHN
ELEMENTARY · SECONDARY · ADULT · LIBRARY

A Harcourt Classroom Education Company

www.steck-vaughn.com

Once upon a time there was a princess.

Her name was Holly.

One night her parents had a feast.

All the king talked about was the fancy food.

All the queen talked about was sewing.

The dancing bear fell asleep in the corner.

Princess Holly yawned.

Then a man began to sing.

"In a castle far away, behind a wall of thorns,
Prince Freddy lies sleeping and dreaming,
Waiting for a brave lass to wake him,
Dreaming of a brave lass to save him."

"I'm a brave lass," Holly said to herself.

"A wall of thorns doesn't scare me."

She ran to the stable where Trixie waited.

They galloped all through the night.

Finally they came to a wall of thorny vines.

Behind the vines Holly could see a castle.

How was she going to get to it?

There was no way to go through the thorns.

A frog named Lilly sat on a leaf.

"There's no way past those thorns," Lilly told Holly.

"I've tried for ten years to get to the castle."

Holly took a rope from her saddle.

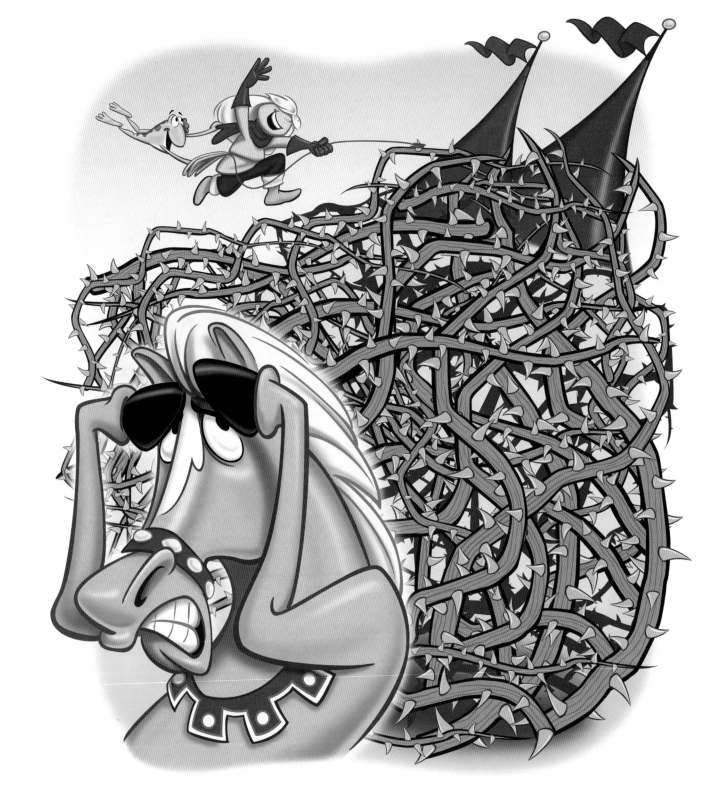

"I'll find a way," Holly told the frog.

Holly swung the rope in a circle.

Then she threw it hard and fast.

The rope stuck, and up Holly went.

"Oh, no. The drawbridge is up," Holly groaned.

"What do we do now?" Lilly asked.

Holly scratched her head.

Then she threw her rope over to a tower.

"Hold on, frog!" cried Holly.

Holly jumped, and they flew across the moat.

Holly and Lilly landed inside a tower window.

Holly dashed down the tower stairs.

Holly raced through every castle tower.

At last she found Prince Freddy fast asleep.

She gave him a good shake.

Nothing happened.

"How do I wake him up?" Holly wondered.

Lilly didn't give her a chance to figure it out.

Lilly gave the prince a big, loud kiss.

Princess Holly stared in surprise.

Poof! A frog sat where Prince Freddy had been!
"Darling!" cried Lilly to Prince Freddy.

"I've waited ten years for your kiss!" Prince
Freddy croaked to Lilly.

13

Together Freddy and Lilly hopped away.

Princess Holly followed them to the moat.

She watched them plop into the water.

Then she watched the castle people wake up.

Princess Holly and Trixie went home.

Holly grew up and visited many castles.

She learned how to climb all kinds of towers.

She even built many castles of her own.

Freddy and Lilly lived happily ever after in the moat.

Every night they gathered up their tadpoles.

They tucked each one in with a kiss.

And then they read them the story of the

princess and the castle.